STRONG

Playing from the Heart WITH

Coco Gauff

by Heather DiLorenzo Williams

FAST READS
full tilt
PRESS

For Lauren, who stood up for what she believed in with passion and strength.

Coco Gauff
TEEN STRONG

Full Tilt Press
42964 Osgood Road
Fremont, CA 94539
readfulltilt.com

Full Tilt Press publications may be purchased for educational, business, or sales promotional use.

Editorial Credits
Design and layout by Sara Radka
Edited by Meghan Gottschall

Image Credits
Al Bello, 12, Al Bello, 27 (top), AYS Sports Marketing/Noam Galai, 20, Cameron Spencer, 23, Clive Brunskill, 4, 13, 18, Dylan Buell, 3, Julian Finney, 25, Kelly Defina, 22, Kevork Djansezian, 29, Lotte New York Palace/Jamie McCarthy, 14, Mitchell Layton, 19, Quinn Rooney, 27 (bottom), Sam Tabone, 24, Shaun Botterill, 9, Stephanie Keith, 16 (bottom), Suzanne Plunkett-Pool, 15; Newscom: AFLO/ PCN/Paul J Sutton, 10, MEGA, 6, 7, 17, 26 (top), ZUMA Press/Panoramic, 11, 26 (bottom), ZUMA Wire/ AFP7/Rob Prange, 8, ZUMA Wire/The Palm Beach Post/Thomas Cordy, 16 (top); Pixabay: Click-Free-Vector-Images, background; Shutterstock: fizkes, 21, lev radin, cover, 1, LHF Graphics, background

ISBN: 978-1-62920-908-1 (library binding)
ISBN: 978-1-62920-912-8 (ePub)

CONTENTS

Introduction

Coco only found out that she would get to play at Wimbledon in 2019 five days before the tournament.

It is a sunny July afternoon in 2019. Cori "Coco" Gauff walks onto the tennis court at Wimbledon in London, England. She is only 15 years old. The teenager was accepted into The Championships, the world's oldest tennis **tournament**, less than a week earlier. One of her most recent accomplishments was passing a high school science test. Now she is facing a four-time Wimbledon champion. In the first **Grand Slam** match of her career, Gauff is playing against one of her tennis idols, Venus Williams.

Coco is nervous as the match begins, hitting Venus's first serve into the net. The point goes to Venus. But the teenager quickly finds her rhythm. The match that follows is fast-paced and intense. For some spectators, it is like watching Venus Williams play her younger self. But Venus cannot keep pace with the teenager, and Coco Gauff defeats her idol. Filled with relief and disbelief, Coco immediately bursts into tears. In that moment, Coco Gauff becomes a superstar.

tournament: a sports competition involving multiple games that ends with a champion

Grand Slam: in tennis, the four most important professional tournaments, which include Wimbledon, the US Open, the Australian Open, and the French Open

Getting Started

Coco has always loved making a fashion statement with bright colors and fun accessories.

Cori Gauff was born on March 13, 2004, in Atlanta, Georgia. She is the oldest child of Corey and Candi Gauff. Both are former college athletes. Corey played basketball at Georgia State University. Candi was a gymnast and ran track at Florida State University. Cori prefers her nickname, Coco. She has two younger brothers named Codey and Cameron.

Becoming a tennis star has not stopped Coco from enjoying simple moments and important traditions with her family.

The Gauffs encouraged all three of their children to try a variety of sports. Coco enjoyed tennis the most. She did not like team sports. According to her dad, she also preferred tennis because she liked wearing a skirt. Corey says his daughter did well in the sport from an early age. She could focus on the court for several minutes at a time. Her parents got her private tennis lessons when she was around six years old.

Coco is the youngest player to qualify for the **main draw** at Wimbledon since 1968.

main draw: the starting lineup in a tennis tournament, reached by winning several qualifying matches

Coco says she often looks for her dad during a match because she knows he will give her a fist pump and encourage her to keep playing hard.

A Family Affair

When Coco was seven, the Gauff family moved to Delray Beach, Florida. Coco's parents grew up there and knew the area would provide more tennis opportunities for their daughter. When she was eight, Coco competed in the "Little Mo" Internationals. This is an international youth tennis tournament named after tennis star Maureen "Little Mo" Connolly Brinker. Coco won first place in the eight-and-under **division**.

At first, Coco just played tennis for fun. She wanted to play with her friends instead of going to tennis practice. But after she won the "Little Mo," she decided to take the game seriously.

Even though she felt like losing was not an option, from an early age, Coco was calm and collected on the court. As former athletes themselves, Coco's parents could see their daughter had a gift. They decided to quit their jobs and focus on her development as a tennis player. Corey became Coco's coach and enrolled her in a local tennis program. Candi, a former teacher, homeschooled Coco so she could have a more flexible schedule. Although they knew it was a risk to give up their jobs for Coco's career, it paid off in the long run.

TENNIS 101

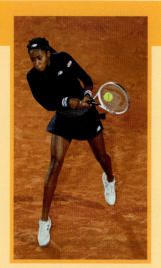

Tennis can be confusing if you've never played. Here are a few basics for beginners:

- There are three main types of tennis courts—clay, grass, and concrete or asphalt. Wimbledon is the only major tournament that is played on a grass court.

- Tennis between two people is called **singles**, and tennis between two pairs is called doubles.

- Most sports play a simple game with a winner or loser. But tennis players play a match made up of multiple sets. Each set contains multiple games. When a player wins six games, that equals one set. To win the whole match, a player usually has to win two out of three sets.

- A player must win at least four points to win a game. Points in tennis are called Love (0), 15 (1), 30 (2), 40 (3), and game point (4). A tied score is called All, and a tie score of 40–40 (or 3–3) is called Deuce. A player must win two points in a row to win the game when the score is Deuce.

division: in sports, a group of teams or athletes who compete against each other
singles: tennis played with one player on each side of the net

Becoming Teen Strong

Coco's ability to stay focused on the tennis court is one of the secrets to her success.

Coaches are always impressed by Coco's unique style. She is very fast and has a powerful serve. She also has the ability to adjust her game depending on her **opponent**. Coaches praise her confidence as well. When Coco was 10, she began training at the Mouratoglou Academy in France. She trained with Serena Williams's longtime coach. His name is Patrick Mouratoglou. "I'll always remember the first time I saw Coco," he said in an interview. He was very impressed by Coco's determination, fighting spirit, and athletic ability. "When she looks at you and tells you she will be number one, you can only believe it," he said.

Coco also started training with a new coach in Florida. His name is Nick Saviano. He has coached several professional tennis stars. Saviano says that Coco is dedicated to becoming one of the world's best players. He also called her **serves** some of the best in the world. During the 2019 US Open, some of Coco's serves were 118 miles (190 kilometers) per hour. Serena Williams has an average serve speed of between 90 and 105 mph (145-169 kph).

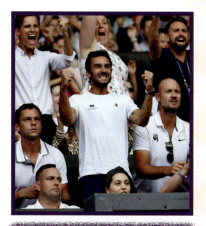

Coach Patrick Mouratoglou says Coco was more mature at age 15 than most players 10 years her senior. He is continually impressed by her unusual self-confidence and inner strength.

Coco is the youngest US Open finalist in the tournament's history.

opponent: a person playing against another person in a sport or contest

serve: the way a ball is put into play in a tennis match by tossing it into the air and hitting it to the other side of the court

A Rising Star

Coco's determination and skill have led to many tournament title wins. In 2017, Coco played her first junior Grand Slam in the US Open. She became the youngest girls' singles finalist in US Open history. She was ranked the number-one Junior player in the world in 2018.

The tennis world started to notice Coco. Many see her as a **successor** for Venus and Serena when they retire from playing. Companies were eager to sponsor her. Coco's **net worth** is already $2.5 million. She has **endorsements** from New Balance, HEAD Tennis, and Barilla pasta. She also partnered with Microsoft to use new tennis technology. This tech may help her improve her game.

Coco has played in more than 20 WTA (Women's Tennis Association) tournaments since 2018. She has one singles title and two doubles titles.

Tennis fans love watching the teenager play. One of her trainers called the 2019 US Open "Cocomania." Thousands of fans chanted "Let's go, Coco!" over and over from the stands. Millions watched her on TV. Coco said she felt like they were cheering for the Golden State Warriors in the NBA championship.

TECHNOLOGY AND TENNIS

Coco is always looking for ways to play better. She began using a new product from Microsoft in 2020. It uses eight high-speed cameras to analyze her body during practice. The 3D cameras produce millions of data points. This data shows every movement Coco makes on the court. Coco can see which movements work best. She and her coaches are able to make adjustments to her game.

successor: a person who has a job or position after someone else

net worth: the value of everything a person owns minus his or her debts

endorsement: an agreement between a company and a person, where the person agrees to publicly support the company or the company's products in exchange for payment

Inspiration

Serena (center) and Venus (right) Williams have praised Coco, calling her hardworking and mature for her age.

Many legendary tennis players have inspired Coco Gauff. One of her favorite players is John Isner. He is known for playing the longest tennis match in history. It lasted a total of 11 hours and 5 minutes. Isner won the match.

But Coco's greatest inspirations are Serena and Venus Williams. Coco was four the first time she saw Serena play. She and her family were watching the 2009 Australian Open. Serena won the singles title, and Venus and Serena won the **doubles** title.

Coco is often compared to the Williams sisters. But she does not think the comparison is fair to Venus and Serena. "I shouldn't be put in the same group yet," she says. "Of course I hope to get where they are," Coco says. The two stars paved the way for girls like Coco to succeed in the sport. For much of her life, Coco had a poster of Serena on her wall. It reminded her to work hard every day.

John Isner set seven other records during his 11-hour match, including most aces in a single match (113) and most games in a single day (118).

Coco is also inspired by Michelle Obama, Beyoncé, and Rihanna.

doubles: tennis played with two players on each side net

Standing Up

Coco is already inspiring others. She says young girls come up to her after matches to tell her they started playing tennis because of her. And she inspires people off the court as well. In June 2020, Coco spoke at a peaceful **protest** in Delray Beach. People were protesting the death of a Black man named George Floyd. Coco talked about how Black people have been fighting for equal treatment for years. "My grandmother was fighting this battle," she said. "Why are we still going through it?"

Coco at Delray Beach

Coco talked about conversations she had with her non-Black friends. She told them that if they liked Black music and culture, then this was their fight too. Coco dedicated her position as a professional athlete to promoting equal rights for Black people. She said she would always use her **platform** to take a stand and fight **racism**. "I'm fighting for the future for my brothers . . . for my future kids . . . for my future grandchildren," she said.

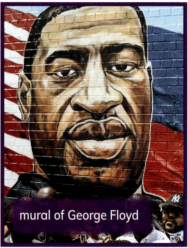
mural of George Floyd

protest: a public objection to an action or policy

platform: the opportunity to share one's beliefs with others

racism: discrimination against a group of people based on skin color or ethnic background

PASSING THE TORCH

Making history is in Coco's blood. When her grandmother Yvonne was 15, she started attending Seacrest High School in Delray Beach. It was 1961, seven years after **segregation** in schools became illegal. She was the school's first and only Black student. Yvonne says she was not nervous. She spoke up in class and even asked to try out for cheerleading. Yvonne passed this confidence on to her granddaughter.

segregation: the separation of people based on skin color

Work in Progress

Coco defeated 19-year-old Anastasia Potapova in the 2019 US Open. Gauff and Potapova made up the youngest first-round matchup in US Open history.

Coco's talent has paved the way to success. But the road has not always been easy. Coco says that being talented from such a young age led to pressure. She felt that she had to improve quickly and win every match.

These feelings eventually led to **anxiety** and **depression**. Coco felt alone even though she had friends and a supportive family. "I was just lost," she said.

Success came with a lot of hype. She rose to the top of her sport quickly. Coco was not prepared for this attention. She almost stopped playing tennis. "I was really depressed," she said. She struggled for an entire year, right up until she **debuted** at Wimbledon. Was playing professionally what she wanted? Or was it what others wanted for her? Coco had a decision to make.

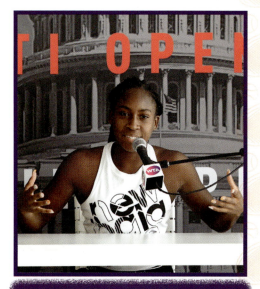

Coco has to maintain confidence on the court as she takes on opponents and off the court as she answers questions from sports writers and reporters.

During her rare moments of free time, Coco loves watching Marvel superhero movies and YouTube makeup tutorials.

anxiety: feelings of worry about what might happen

depression: a state of deep sadness that does not go away over time

debut: to do something in public for the first time

Overcoming Obstacles

Coco realized that she had to start playing for herself and not for other people. Although she has been called the next Serena Williams, Coco is her own person with her own unique style. When she decided to play for herself, she fell in love with tennis even more.

Learning to manage the stress and pressure in her life helped Coco become an even better player. "It took many moments sitting, thinking, and crying," Coco says. But choosing to keep playing felt right to Coco. Her attitude on the court became more positive. She says she came through the difficult year more thankful to be playing tennis. Coco knew herself better than ever before, and it showed.

After months of soul-searching, Coco rediscovered the joy of playing tennis and started playing with new energy and enthusiasm.

"Once I let go, that's when I started to have the results I wanted," Coco says. Coco started winning like never before. Around this same time, she got a **wildcard** spot at Wimbledon. Her performance in that tournament was proof that she had made the right choice.

GETTING HELP WITH ANXIETY OR DEPRESSION

Feeling depressed or anxious is common among teens. Dealing with school, social, or family stress can be difficult. Sometimes exercise can improve sad or anxious feelings. Eating balanced meals, drinking enough water, and getting at least eight hours of sleep can help too. Having someone to talk to is also important. But sometimes these feelings don't easily get better. Sometimes teens need help from a counselor or therapist. This is a person who can offer strategies for understanding and **coping** with severe anxiety and depression.

wildcard: in tennis, a spot in a tournament awarded by the tournament's organizers

coping: dealing with something using various methods

A Bright Future

After losing to Naomi Osaka in straight sets in the 2019 US Open, Coco celebrated her victory over the reigning champion in the third round of the 2020 Australian Open.

Coco turned 17 in March 2021. At that age, many teens might be getting a car and hanging out with friends. Coco was making history. In 2019, she became the youngest player to win a match in the Wimbledon main draw since 1991. She was ranked in the top 50 tennis players in the world. By the time she turned 16, she had won a major singles title. She is the youngest WTA singles title winner since 2004.

Naomi Osaka has won four Grand Slam titles, including the US Open in both 2018 and 2020.

Coco has beaten some of the best-known players in the world. She defeated Venus Williams at Wimbledon in 2019. She beat her again a few months later at the Australian Open. She also defeated Naomi Osaka at the Australian Open. Osaka was the defending champion of the tournament and one of the top five players in the world. Coco is the youngest

Coco's four Wimbledon appearances were ESPN's most-watched matches on the days she played in the tournament.

person to beat a top-five player since 1991. At the 2021 Australian Open, Coco reached the second round in the singles competition. She and her doubles partner Caty McNally reached the quarterfinals.

Going the Distance

For Coco, being the best is a given. She is fully dedicated to becoming the top player in the world. But she wants to do it on her terms. "I'm not going to be the next Serena Williams," she said. "I am going to be the first Cori 'Coco' Gauff."

Being Coco Gauff means making hard choices and staying focused on her goals. She knows she will have to say no to things other teens say yes to. And she will have to say yes to things most teens don't even think about. It also means using her platform to make the world a better place, whether she's posting a tribute to Dr. Martin Luther King Jr., or speaking to a crowd about racial justice.

Coco attended an event in Melbourne, Australia, to welcome tennis stars to the 2020 Australia Open. The following week, she beat Naomi Osaka, the reigning champion.

Her coaches and family believe this one-of-a-kind player can go the distance. And although her journey hasn't always been easy, Coco believes it too. With a strong serve, a strong spirit, and a strong voice, Coco will take the tennis court and the world by storm.

THE WILLIAMS SISTERS

Venus and Serena Williams are two of the best-known tennis players in the world. They grew up playing tennis. Serena became a **professional** player when she was just 14 years old. Venus has won more than 45 **titles**, and Serena has more than 70. The sisters have faced each other on the court more than 30 times. The Williams sisters are known for their intense play and their unique styles on the court. Venus also has a fashion degree from the Art Institute of Fort Lauderdale in Florida.

professional: in sports, an athlete who is paid to play rather than one who plays as a pastime

title: in sports, the status as the champion in a competition

Timeline

March 13, 2004

Coco is born in Atlanta, Georgia.

2009

Coco becomes interested in tennis after seeing Serena Williams play in the Australian Open.

2014

Coco begins training with Patrick Mouratoglou in France and goes on to win the USTA Clay Court National.

2017

Coco begins playing in the ITF Junior Circuit at age 13.

May 2018

Coco makes her debut in the ITF Women's Circuit and wins her first professional match.

2019

In her first appearance at Wimbledon, Coco defeats one of her longtime idols, Venus Williams.

2020

At a peaceful protest in Delray Beach, Florida, Coco speaks to a crowd about racial justice and equality following the death of George Floyd earlier in the summer.

2021

Coco makes it to the second round in the singles competition at the Australian open, her best performance since she began playing in the tournament in 2019.

QUIZ

#1

How old was Coco when she first saw Serena Williams play tennis?

#2

During what year was Coco ranked the number-one junior player in the world?

#3

Why did Coco's family move to Florida when she was seven?

#4

Who are Coco's biggest inspirations outside of tennis?

#5

Whom does Coco say she is fighting against racial inequality and injustice for in her June 2020 speech?

#6

What legendary men's tennis player won the longest tennis match in history?

6. John Isner

5. Her brothers, future children, and future grandchildren

4. Michelle Obama, Beyoncé, and Rihanna

3. There were more opportunities to play tennis.

2. 2018

1. Four

ACTIVITY

Coco is not the first young athlete to take the sports world by storm. Swimmer Michael Phelps competed in the Olympics at age 15. Mia Hamm was 15 when she debuted on the US Women's National Soccer Team. Kobe Bryant was the youngest person to ever start in an NBA game. What made these athletes Teen Strong?

STEPS

1. Research another teen athlete—it could be one mentioned here, or another that you discover in your research.

2. Use these questions to guide your research. You can come up with others too.

   - Where did the athlete grow up? What was their family like?
   - When did the athlete start playing the sport they're known for?
   - What major sporting events has the athlete competed in?
   - What are some unique traits/interesting facts about the athlete?

3. Write a brief biography of the athlete OR create an artistic poster that tells about their life.

GLOSSARY

anxiety: feelings of worry about what might happen

coping: dealing with something using various methods

debut: to do something in public for the first time

depression: a state of deep sadness that does not go away over time

division: in sports, a group of teams or athletes who compete against each other

doubles: tennis played with two players on each side net

endorsement: an agreement between a company and a person, where the person agrees to publicly support the company or the company's products in exchange for payment

Grand Slam: in tennis, the four most important professional tournaments, which include Wimbledon, the US Open, the Australian Open, and the French Open

main draw: the starting lineup in a tennis tournament, reached by winning several qualifying matches

net worth: the value of everything a person owns minus his or her debts

opponent: a person playing against another person in a sport or contest

platform: the opportunity to share one's beliefs with others

professional: in sports, an athlete who is paid to play rather than one who plays as a pastime

protest: a public objection to an action or policy

racism: discrimination against a group of people based on skin color or ethnic background

segregation: the separation of groups of people based on skin color

serve: the way a ball is put into play in a tennis match by tossing it into the air and hitting it to the other side of the court

singles: tennis played with one player on each side of the net

successor: a person who has a job or position after someone else

title: in sports, the status as the champion in a competition

tournament: a sports competition involving multiple games or matches that ends with a champion

wildcard: in tennis, a spot in a tournament awarded by the tournament's organizers

READ MORE

Dufresne, Emilie. *Tennis.* New York: KidHaven Publishing, 2020.

Wetzel, Dan. *Serena Williams.* New York: Henry Holt and Company, 2019.

Zuckerman, Gregory, et al. *Rising Above: Inspiring Women in Sports.* New York: Puffin Books, 2019.

Zullo, Allan. *10 True Tales: Young Civil Rights Heroes.* New York: Scholastic, 2019.

INTERNET SITES

https://www.ducksters.com/sports/tennis.php
Learn how tennis is played, with links to basic rules, strategies, and a tennis glossary.

https://www.ducksters.com/sports/professional_tennis.php
Explore the world of professional tennis, including major tournaments, rankings, and how professional players earn money.

https://kidshealth.org/en/kids/depression.html?WT.ac=ctg#catemotion
Learn more about sadness and depression in kids and teens, including tips for coping and ways to get help.

https://www.usopen.org/en_US/players/overview/wta328560.html
Explore a statistical overview of Coco Gauff's professional tennis career.

INDEX